THE DARK MEADOW

ANDREA MARIA SCHENKEL

Translated from the German by Anthea Bell

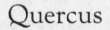

Published in Germany as *Finsterau* by Hoffmann & Campe
First published in Great Britain in 2014 by Quercus Editions
This paperback edition published in 2015 by

Quercus Publishing Ltd
Carmelite House
50 Victoria Embankment
London EC4Y 0DZ

An Hachette UK company

A CIP catalogue record for this book is available
from the British Library

PB ISBN 978 1 78087 776 1
EBOOK ISBN 978 1 78087 775 4

10 9 8 7 6 5 4 3

Typeset by Ellipsis Digital Limited, Glasgow

Printed and bound in Great Britain by Clays Ltd, St Ives plc

THE DARK MEADOW

Hermann Müller

Roswitha Haimerl stood there with her coat buttoned up and her bag under her arm. 'I'm off home now, Hermann. I've cleared up the bar and stood the chairs on the tables, except for the one at the corner table. There's some no-good layabout still sitting there, he'll have to throw himself out. He's paid what he owes.'

'Steady. You can't be sure he's a drifter just because he looks like one. But off you go. We'll be busy tomorrow, the regulars will be back.'

The landlord was just rinsing out the last glasses. He put them on the draining rack beside the sink to dry and wiped his damp hands on the dish towel.

'Oh, and before I forget, I was going to ask if you can get here a little earlier.'

'Yes, that's OK. See you tomorrow, then.'

Roswitha Haimerl went to the door. Hermann Müller accompanied her.

'Good night, and mind you don't let anyone pick you up.'

'Don't you worry, Hermann, if anyone comes to meet me at night he'll bring me back next morning at the latest. So long, and make sure you get rid of that no-good fellow.'

Roswitha Haimerl went away, laughing, while the landlord locked up behind her. He left the key in the lock. Then he went over to the corner table.

The guest lay with his torso slumped over the table, one hand under his face, the other holding his half-full beer glass. The landlord picked up the glass and put it out of the sleeping man's reach. Then he placed a hand on his shoulder and tried to wake him.

'Hey, time to go home. We're closing. Can you hear me?'

The man, obviously muzzy, straightened up. 'OK, OK, just going.'

'Want me to get you a taxi? Or can you walk home?'

The stranger tried to stand up, slipped, and fell back on the chair. 'You let me be! Like I said, I'm just going. Take your great paws off of me!'

'Go easy, go easy. Like me to help you?'

'I don't need no help, I don't.'

He tried to get to his feet again, clinging to the table top with both hands. As he did so his key ring fell to the floor.

Hermann Müller bent down and picked the keys up. 'Tell you what, I'm getting you a taxi. You can't drive in that state, friend! Or the police will pick you up, and I'll be in the shit for not calling a taxi.'

'The police, what a laugh!' And indeed, the guest tried laughing. 'You think they care? Someone's had one over the eight, oh yes, they'll stick their oar in then, they'll take him in, the police will, but murder someone and they don't give a damn. It's all one to them, I'm telling you.'

'What are you babbling on about? What's all right to who?'

Somehow or other the drunk had managed to get to his feet. He leaned slightly forward, swaying, and brought his face close to the landlord's.

'The police let murderers go free, let me tell you that.'

He kept tapping the landlord's chest with his forefinger.

'I know about a murder. Two years after the war, that was, and no one wants to know. But *I* know, and I'm not letting it rest. I know who done it and why. But *they* don't want to know a thing about it.'

'I can't think that the police don't want to know about a murder.'

'Them? They don't want to know a thing, not a thing. It's all the same to them, they don't care. Never even investigated properly, they didn't.' He put his forefinger to his mouth. 'Ssh! Not a word, got to keep mum! Oh yes, I know all about it.'

He dropped back on the chair again.

'See, it's like with them three monkeys. See no evil, speak no evil, hear no evil. And if it looks like foreign cops got to be brought in, they don't want to touch it. Better keep their mouths shut than call the Frenchies in. Don't want to show themselves up, do they?'

'That's a load of garbage. Why would the police do nothing just to avoid making inquiries abroad?'

But the man did not reply; his head was down on the table again and he was asleep. Hermann Müller had another shot at waking him, but after a while he abandoned the attempt, put out the light, shot the bolt on the door of the bar, picked up the day's takings and went home to his apartment upstairs.

Next morning the man had gone. Some time during the night he had climbed out of a window in the bar, leaving his wallet lying under the table.

When Roswitha Haimerl came to get the bar ready for the day, she found a few till receipts and a twenty-mark note in the wallet, along with a yellowed old newspaper cutting. Her curiosity aroused, she unfolded it.

'Take a look at this, Hermann. Don't you know him? Surely that's Dr Augustin!'

She held the news report out to the landlord. 'In that picture – he was still young then.'

The landlord took the cutting. 'Let's see it.'

Then he folded it up again and put it in his own wallet.

'Tell you what, Roswitha, I'll show that cutting to Augustin when he comes in for his usual at midday. What a joke! Can't wait to hear what he says, especially when I tell him the story of that layabout drunk yesterday.'

Afra

The shutters had been half open all night, letting out the sultry heat of the day and allowing the cooler morning air to stream into the room. The mosquito came in with it, and now its high-pitched whine has woken her. Afra lies in her bed in the bedroom, listening. The sound gets louder when the insect comes closer, fainter when it moves away. Sometimes it even flies so close to her face that she feels a slight current of air on her skin. Afra lies there quietly, waiting. The humming gets louder and finally stops. She feels the mosquito on her cheek, keeps still a moment longer, then hits out with the flat of her hand. The insect's body, swollen with blood, bursts, and the sticky fluid clings to her fingers and her cheek.

*

Afra opens her eyes. Disgusted, she wipes her hand on the sheet. The light in the room is grey. The few pieces of furniture are dark shapes standing out against the walls. Just before sunrise. Time to get up. She pushes the quilt aside; feeling the cold trodden-mud floor under her bare feet, she sits on the edge of the bed a little longer, looking across the room at Albert, who is asleep in his cot. The child is dear to her, and at the same time a stranger. He is her flesh and blood, so she must love him, but sometimes, when she's sitting on her bed as she is now, she wishes he wasn't there. Then her life would be simpler. She instantly feels ashamed, tells herself it's unfair and sinful to think like that, the child can't help it, and there are good moments too, she wouldn't want to miss those. All the same, she can't shake off the thought; it torments her, it comes back again and again. There are only a few days when she's entirely free of it. Yesterday was one of them. Her parents went to Mass early, and on after that to visit relations. Afra and the child stayed behind in the house on their own. All that day, she'd felt none of the nightmare pressure that usually weighed down on her. To get out of going with her parents she had said there was laundry to do, the whites needed washing, and in spite of the drudgery it had been her best Sunday in a long time. She'd got up at four in the morning, had breakfast and went out into the yard.

Before the others in the house were awake, she was already standing at the wooden trough, taking out the things that had been soaking in soda overnight and rubbing them on the washboard one by one. When she had put the big pan containing the laundry and soft soap on the kitchen stove, her father and mother had just been getting ready to go to church. Once they had left, she woke Albert and dressed him, did the housework, and from time to time she stirred the boiling washing with the big wooden kitchen spoon. The little boy ran about energetically, and she had been afraid he might scald himself on the hot soapsuds in a careless moment. So in the end she had taken him on her lap, and together they sang the song about the little witch who gets up at six in the morning to go into the barn. They sang it over and over again, until it was time to take the washing out of the suds and rub it on the washboard in the yard again. Albert never tired of helping as far as he could. He carried the smaller items over to the trough to rinse them in cold water from the well until he was wet all over, and his hands were blue with cold. Afra took his wet clothes off, dried him, and sat him down with a piece of bread on the bench in the sun outside the house. And when she had finally wrung out the washing and spread it on the meadow to bleach, she too sat down in the sun and watched the little boy trying to drive the neighbour's geese away with a thin switch, to keep them from walking all over the laundry on the ground. From time to time she stood up and went to sprinkle the washing lying out to bleach with water, until finally she put it all back in the tub in the evening, ready to be hung out to dry next morning.

When she was clearing everything up and was about to go indoors with the boy, two travelling journeymen came by the yard and asked if she knew where they could stay the night. One of them reminded her slightly of Albert's father; it wasn't so much his looks as the way he smiled when his eyes dwelt on her. She had talked to them for a little while, and then sent them over to the neighbour's house. After that she had gone indoors with the child to make supper. While she was busy with that, Albert had fallen asleep on the sofa in the kitchen, and she carried the sleeping child over to the bedroom without waking him.

Afra takes a deep breath. Why can't every day be as carefree as yesterday? Then she gets up, dresses herself quietly so as not to wake Albert, and goes into the kitchen.

Day is beginning to dawn at last outside the window. She hesitates: should she put the light on in the kitchen? With her hand already on the switch she decides not to, and in the dim light she goes over to the cubbyhole where kindling is kept beside the stove, takes matches, paper, twigs and pieces of wood, opens the stove door and gets the fire going. Then she lifts the wooden bowl down from the shelf and goes into the pantry. The earthenware basin of milk set out to curdle is standing on the windowsill. Afra ladles curds out of it into the smaller wooden bowl. Fills it to the brim. Carefully, making sure she doesn't spill any, she goes back into the kitchen. There she puts the bowl of curds for breakfast on the table, with some bread to break into it. Afra takes a spoon out of the table drawer and puts it down beside the bowl. She sits there waiting. Her father or mother could open the kitchen door any moment now. She can imagine what it will be like when they come in. Her mother will be telling her off again for not going to church yesterday, and not to Evensong either, saying how ashamed she felt in front of the whole village and their relations. Her father will tell her to sit like a good girl and say a morning prayer of thanksgiving with him.

She will feel bad. Ever since she was little they've made her feel she has done something wrong, or was in the wrong place at the wrong time. She can't do anything right in her parents' eyes. She knows how hard her mother takes it if she doesn't say prayers and go to church. But she doesn't want to, she won't. Is she supposed to feel grateful for having to fight for the simplest things all over again every day? Who is this God of theirs who forces such a life on her? She hates the poverty, the cramped conditions here. But most of all she can't stand her parents' slavish regard for authority. All that, 'What will people say, child? Haven't you brought enough shame on us? Why can't you tread the straight and narrow road of righteousness?'

Angrily, she pushes the bowl aside with a jerk, ignoring the curdled milk slopping over, and stands up.

At that moment her father comes into the kitchen. Afra doesn't look at him, doesn't wish him good morning, makes her way past him.

'Where do you think you're going? Doesn't anyone say good morning in this house any more? This is a place where decent people still live!' he calls after her.

She replies quietly, without turning to look at him, 'Oh, get lost, you old fool.'

Johann

They hadn't let him go. He ought to have known, it was like that other time, back then. He'd spent his whole life trying to be God-fearing and respectable. Just like before, they'd taken him away and wouldn't let him go again.

That boy, he'd always been getting underfoot, he was always in the way. And as for her, she'd spoilt him. It hadn't been right of her. Hadn't been right.

He paced up and down the cell, he couldn't sit down. He couldn't think straight, either.

Take up thy cross daily and follow me. The only difference was why. When it happened before, it had been his faith. He wouldn't abjure it. He had stood firmly by his God.

'Yea, though I walk through the valley of the shadow of death ... though I walk through the valley of the shadow of death ...'

How did it go on? He couldn't remember.

There was so much he couldn't remember any more. It annoyed him, why was he suddenly so confused these days? He was beginning to mislay things, or find himself somewhere without knowing what he wanted to do there, or even where he was. Then he sat down and waited until it came back into his mind. Maybe they were right, and it had been him, but he wasn't crazy. He stood up and went on walking around the cell.

They'd kept him for eight weeks that other time, and in the end they'd let him go. He hadn't abjured, he had held fast to his faith. Ever since the day when he made his vow he had stood firmly by it. He could remember that, he wasn't forgetful, and didn't that prove it? It was all there, every detail, clear and distinct as if it had been only yesterday. He'd joined the Third Order even before the First World War. He'd been a young fellow at the time, and he had sworn to himself to lead a God-fearing life. Ever since then, he had worn the cord around his body as a sign of his membership of the Order. In the last year of the war he had married Theres. Her brothers had all fallen fighting, and her father and mother were long dead. She had no one now, and it was time he looked for a wife. Love comes with marriage. From then on they went through life together. She was no beauty, small, always too thin, but she was devout and modest. She'd already had four children before Afra was born, none of them survived more than two days, one was born dead before its time, another died while she was in labour. He began to doubt whether it had been right for them to marry, because they were blood relations, although at some distance. When they neither of them still expected God to give them a child, Afra came into the world. And then, from the first day on, it seemed as if the Lord wanted to test their faith by giving them a child like Afra. Afra had ideas of her own, she told lies, she went on lying even when he caught her at it. She brought him nothing but trouble. Was flirting with the boys from the neighbourhood at an early age. He beat her to make her stay on the straight and narrow path. She didn't care, shook herself like a wet dog, and he suspected Theres of comforting her behind his back. As soon as Afra had finished school she went away. She very seldom came home, and if she did, it wasn't for long. But she couldn't have stayed in the house anyway. They had nothing, only just enough to live on. He worked on the railway, Theres sat at her sewing machine until late at night making edgings and braid for the farmers' wives' Sunday-best clothes. Although he thought poorly of their addiction to finery, customers came from all over the place, and they could do with every pfennig.

He walked and walked, he didn't want to stop. He couldn't remember the rest of the psalm, which made him furious. Why did it go out of his mind just now? He had always followed the path of righteousness. Always followed the straight and narrow path, all his life. He had prayed and worked, tried to be a good man and bring up his daughter in the fear of the Lord. He always knew his place, only once had he refused to obey authority, and he'd paid for that. Just after that brown-shirted gang came to power. He'd felt abandoned at the time, even the priest in the pulpit parroted what those folk said. But he went on reading the Bible every evening with his wife and child, so he couldn't keep his mouth shut, he stood up before everyone and openly contradicted the priest, in front of the whole congregation. He had said that no upright Christian could be glad of what was happening, they'd all be led into misfortune, the priest and the bishop couldn't allow it.

They came the very next day and took him away. He could remember Afra, still a small child at the time, standing beside her mother in the doorway. He could even say what clothes they were both wearing then. Yes, he remembered Theres stroking Afra's head as the two of them stood there, watching him being taken away in the car.

They had taken him away and questioned him.

After eight weeks they'd let him go again. He survived the beatings, the mockery, the hunger and all the rest of the harassment, because the Lord God was with him. Before they let him go, he had to sign something saying he wouldn't breathe a word to anyone about what he had seen, what he now knew, or they would come for him again, and this time they'd never let him go. And he hadn't said a word about it to a living soul. Not even his wife. He forbade himself even to think of it, he rooted it out of his memory, for fear they might come back for him again. He kept his mouth shut, he learned never to protest, never to rebel again.

'Yea, though I walk through the valley of the shadow of death ...'

He couldn't remember. However hard he tried, the memory was gone. As if he had a big, black hole in his head, and if he didn't watch out, even for a moment, it would swallow up all his thoughts and memories. He went on walking up and down, bracing his mind against oblivion.

Afra

Three years ago almost to the day, in the summer of 1944, Afra had returned to her parental home. There she was at the door with an old bicycle and her few possessions. She had turned up, just like that, without previous warning. They hadn't seen her at home for years. At the age of fourteen, right after school, she'd left. First she worked as a kitchen skivvy, then as a maid and a waitress. In all those years she went home three or maybe four times at the most, only to leave again as soon as possible. She wasn't homesick, not even at first, and she never wanted to go back. But then the day came when she had to leave her job in a hurry. Her employer had thrown her out in disgrace, and she went like a beaten dog.

'And you just be glad to get off so lightly,' he had called

after her as she left. 'A tart sleeping around with Frenchmen and foreigners! A dirty whore, that's what you are, a slut! I can't be doing with the likes of you here.'

He'd even kept back a large part of the wages still owing to her.

That was the same evening as she had found the letter, although she couldn't really be said to have 'found' it: she couldn't possibly have missed it, since the upright and honest folk of the village had nailed it to the inside of her bedroom door. So when she closed the door and was going to hang up her overall on the nail behind the door as usual, the hate letter instantly met her eyes. They'd hang her from the nearest tree, it said, she ought to creep away from here, right away would be best. She was a disgrace to all honest German women whose husbands were fighting in the war, it said. She was a dirty whore, and she'd better watch out, because they'd be waiting for her, and then God help her.

Afra tore the scrap of paper off the door and ran down to the taproom. Trembling all over with rage, she threw the note down on the bar, smoothed it out flat with both hands and held it down as if a gust of wind might blow it away. She wanted to ask the landlord if she hadn't always worked hard and conscientiously.

'Haven't I worked like a horse here? What's the idea of this?'

But he cut her short and simply grunted, 'They'll be right, those folks. A cow like you ought to creep away. And better today than tomorrow. Understand? Better for us all that way, I can't have a tart like you in my house. The disgrace of it'll rub off on me, or they'll lock me up for not reporting you. No need to look so fierce. I'll tell you one thing, I'm not taking no risks for a girl like you – I could end up in a camp. Got to look out for number one, me. I can't manage without them Frenchies, but I can do without a tart like you. I need everyone who can lend a hand on the land or in the house. A man that's not afraid of hard work. It don't make no difference to me where he comes from, and that Frenchman costs as good as nothing. So now off you go, and I don't want to find you still here in the morning.'

With these words he turned round and left her alone. Afra went up to her room, packed all her possessions, and left. The landlady threw some money at her feet when she asked about her wages. Coins rolled all over the taproom floor. She scrambled around on her knees, picking up the money. The landlord himself had refused to see her. And they burned the letter she had left for the Frenchman that same evening. Why hand it over? When the foreign workers were brought in tomorrow morning Afra would be gone, and everything could go its usual way again, much better for everyone.

She spent three days and two nights on her journey. She cycled until she was exhausted and then pushed the bike, and when she couldn't go any further she stopped for a short break on the outskirts of a wood or by a spring of water if she happened to pass one. She rented a place to sleep the first night at a little inn, and set off again as soon as the sun rose. She found a place in the hay on the second night. And then, late in the afternoon, she suddenly saw Finsterau ahead of her. Her parents' house was even smaller and shabbier than she remembered it. Two bedrooms, one even tinier than the other, a kitchen and the pantry. The windows were draughty holes, and even in summer the place had a damp, musty smell. Water had to be pumped up from the well in the yard and carried indoors, and the outside lavatory was next to the dung heap. The sewage system hadn't yet reached the outskirts of the village here, and even if it had her parents couldn't have afforded it, not before the war when times were better, still less now. At least electricity cables had been laid at the beginning of the twenties, just after Afra had been born. Her mother was so proud of it that she sat at her sewing machine all night. Sewing on spangles to earn a little on the side, since Afra's father worked on the railways, first as a day labourer, then as a platelayer. Earning too much to die on and too little to live on, as they say. They were poor cottagers. She'd wanted to get away from all that poverty, she had run away from home back then, only to return now. So she stood there in the yard looking around. As usual, the door of the house was wide open, and the white bucket with the ladle stood beside the door. Since her earliest childhood it had been her job to fill the bucket with fresh water from the well. Nothing had changed, nothing was going to change, time had stood still in this place.

'For ever and ever, amen.'

And, as if she had never been away, Afra picked up the bucket and went over to the well.

In April '45 the war reached this part of the country, and then it ended in May, and Albert was born only a little later. She hadn't noticed that she was pregnant by the Frenchman until she was back at home. For her strictly devout parents he was a disgrace, a child of sin. And as if to emphasize his birth out of wedlock even further, that afternoon a storm broke out of a clear sky, making the day into night. Her mother put the black storm candle in the window and prayed fervently and in a loud voice for God to avert the storm while her grandson was being born in the next room. At first Afra still believed the Frenchman would come back for them after the war was over. After all, in her goodbye letter she had told him where she was going, but when her hopes came to nothing the memory of him steadily faded. While at first she could still remember every detail, the images in her head turned pale, like clothes that had often been washed, and finally disappeared entirely. First his face went. One day she found herself unable, with the best will in the world, to say what colour his eyes were, although only recently they had still been present in her mind. His mouth, his nose, everything disappeared, and in the end only a pale, empty surface was left. Then she also forgot the sound of his voice, the way he held himself, the way he walked; it was as if he had been extinguished. The smell of him lingered longest, but one day even the memory of that was gone.

If it hadn't been for Albert, she would never have wasted another thought on him, just as you forgot the dream you had in the night even before you woke up next morning. But Albert was here, and their situation in the house became more intolerable every day.

**From the evidence of the police officer
Hermann Irgang, now retired,
eighteen years after the events concerned**

First thing I'd like to say is this happened almost twenty years ago — if I say
something then that's the way I remember
it, but I can't tell you every detail, not
now. At the time I was first on the scene
of the crime, with my colleague Weinzierl.

Their neighbour, Schlegler, came to us at
the station at the time and said, 'There's
been an accident in the cottagers' house
out there.'

Schlegler couldn't say what exactly had
happened, because the old man had come to
him talking all confused stuff. All he could
make out was that something was wrong with

Afra and the child. He, the neighbour, was supposed to run and fetch the police. Zauner himself went home again.

We village policemen didn't have a police car in those days. It was just after the war, and we all went about on bikes. You couldn't do that nowadays.

Weinzierl was new to the force, he'd applied to join only a few months before. I thought I'd take him with me, so as he'd learn something and get to know the people and the district better. So we went together by bike.

From outside the place looked quite normal. Washing was hanging on the line beside the house. I still remember that washing vividly because there'd seemed to be a storm brewing all morning, so I was surprised no one had taken it off the line yet.

When we were in the kitchen I thought Zauner looked suspicious right away. He was standing there bending over the washbasin. He hadn't even turned his head to the door, although he'd heard us coming. His body was scrawny, sinewy — you could see he'd worked like a horse all his life. He just stood there in his undershirt and trousers. His braces were hanging down on both sides, his undershirt was dirty and sweaty. He was holding a wet rag. Only when we came closer could we see that it wasn't a rag at all, it was his shirt. It was soaked with blood and water. It was clear to us he'd been trying to wash the blood out. There was no other explanation.

I'd expected the old man to be upset and agitated, from all we'd heard from Schlegler. But he just stood there in the kitchen like it was nothing to do with him. He was splashing the water about; he didn't stop until I told him to sit down. He went over to the chair and sat down without a word. Sat there with his legs apart, looking stubborn. I took the shirt from his hand. He didn't register that, just went on staring ahead of him. Zauner wasn't shedding tears, wasn't desperate. Nothing. He just sat there looking at his hands as if nothing had happened.

If my daughter and my grandson had an accident, I wouldn't stand there at the basin washing, would I? That's not what any normal person does.

As a village policeman you get to hear this and that, and we'd heard from all over the district that those folks in the shepherd's cottage didn't get on well together. The old man and Afra, they were like cat and dog. He'd always been quarrelsome, and it got worse every year.

The child in particular was a thorn in his flesh. Right, so it's a disgrace for her to have a child out of wedlock. But she wasn't the first to have a bastard, and she wouldn't be the last. To this day I don't know how you can fly off the handle about it like that.

Afra

Afra slips into the clogs standing beside the door of the house and goes out into the yard. The tub of bleached laundry is standing on the bench outside the house. She picks it up with both hands and carries it over to the well. There she rinses the whites again in the open air. Her hands soon turn red in the cold water, and hurt at every movement. Item by item, she wrings them out as well as she can on the rim of the stone trough. Then she puts them in the basket. From time to time she straightens up, dries her hands on her apron, and tries to warm her stiff, cold fingers by rubbing them together. As she does so she glances at the door, and sees her father come out of the house. He doesn't even look her way. There is just one sheet still lying in the water, she rinses it through, and when she has wrung out this last item and put it in the basket, her mother too comes out of the house and goes straight over to Afra.

'I have to go over to Einhausen, and then to the Müllers. You'll be here alone with your father most of the time.'

And without waiting for any reply, she goes on, 'I'll see that I get back early in the afternoon. I've just looked at Albert, he's lying in bed asleep still, but it won't be long before he wakes up. Your father has gone to mow the meadow beside the railway embankment. Mind you don't go quarrelling with him again when I'm not here – the neighbours can hear you arguing the whole time, no need for the rest of the village to know as well. I couldn't get a wink of sleep last night, it takes so much out of me. I want an end to the hostility in this house at last.'

'It won't be my fault if there isn't, Mother.'

'I don't care whose fault it is. I want some peace and quiet, and that's that.'

She turns without another word, goes over to her bicycle, jams her basket on the carrier, and just before she rides away she calls to Afra again, 'Your father will be back in two hours' time – you must get him his mid-morning snack. He's hungry when he comes home from mowing, so mind you think of that and don't forget it!'

Afra stands there with the laundry basket in her hand, and says in a quiet voice with a bitter undertone, more to herself than anyone else, 'Oh no, I won't forget it.'

She goes past the house to the larger wooden shed. She puts up the washing line from the back wall of the shed, stretching it over to the house. Takes the laundry out of the basket and hangs it on the line. When she has finished she leans the laundry basket against the shed, goes to the smaller shed, which is the chicken house, opens the door and lets the fowls out into the garden. She watches as they scurry over to the fruit trees or disappear under the currant bushes. She loves standing here and looking at the garden. The sight of the trees in blossom in spring is her favourite, especially when the wind blows the white petals over the meadow like snowflakes. As a child she made herself a camp under the bushes in the other corner of the garden. Whenever she could get out of the house, she would sit here behind the bushes, playing. Afra goes over to her old hiding-place, and she thinks she sees something glinting in the grass. At first she isn't sure, wonders whether she was mistaken, but then she sees it again right at the end of the garden, something lying in the meadow close to the stinging nettles. Once she gets to the place, she can't find it at first. She bends down, wraps the fabric of the apron round her hand, and carefully parts the stinging nettles. The small hoe lies there in the grass in front of her. Her absent-minded father will have left it there, and when he next looks for it and can't find it he will blame her for losing it. He is becoming forgetful, and says the same things all over again, three or four times running. At meals, he often finds it hard to carry a spoon to his mouth without spilling the soup in it. If Afra or her mother tell him not to act like that he gets cross and picks a quarrel. Recently he has been flying into a rage about everything and nothing, with a degree of violence that surprises and at the same time alarms everyone. Afra reaches for the hoe, picks it up, and goes back to the shed. The wet, heavy sheets hang from the washing line, moving back and forth lazily in the slight breeze. A white wall of fabric, bellying out and then collapsing again.

Johann

All that Johann Zauner could remember later was Afra lying face up on the sofa. Her eyes were open, and broken glass was scattered over the floor. He had trodden on the glass – even long afterwards he remembered the noise when he did that. The crunch as he ground the glass under the soles of his shoes. He stood there, and didn't understand what had happened. He saw that her hair was beginning to go red with the blood that was slowly seeping into the sofa. With a trembling hand, he touched her forehead, passed his hand tenderly over her lids and closed her eyes.

It was only then that he heard the whimpering. He felt as if it were abruptly rousing him from a dream. He looked around enquiringly, and finally he found the child lying on the floor, half covered by the chair that had fallen over. He pushed the chair aside, awkwardly helped the little boy up and held him tightly. Very tightly, not the way you hold a child, more like a bundle of rags when you have to take care not to let any scraps of fabric drop out.

'Don't be scared, it will be all right, it will be all right,' he kept saying again and again.

He spoke only to hear a calming voice, and so as not to feel alone.

With the whimpering child held to his chest, he went out into the yard. Both arms firmly round the bundle, he set off to go over to the neighbour's house. He had gone half the way before he noticed something wet and warm running through his fingers and down his arms. And when he stopped and looked down at himself, he saw the blood. He didn't know what to do, and waited a moment. He took a few steps forward, then a few more in the opposite direction, and finally he turned and went slowly back to the house.

In the kitchen, he pushed the broken glass and the hoe lying on the floor aside, and laid the child carefully on the floor beside the sofa. He didn't want to put the boy down beside his dead mother, there wasn't enough room, and he was afraid that he might make an incautious movement, fall off the sofa and hurt himself. And he couldn't bring himself to touch Afra again. He fetched the old woollen shawl from the bedroom and covered the child with it. He was afraid the little boy might catch his death of cold, lying on the floor like that.

At some time he must have gone over to the neighbour's. They said he had called to him over the fence, telling him to get in touch with the police. Or at least, that was what the police officers told him later. He didn't remember it himself. If memory is a vessel full to the brim with what you had experienced, then his was broken like the pieces of the glass bottle in the kitchen that he had trodden on. His memories were fragments, with gaps between them that couldn't be filled; on many days he could no longer distinguish between what was real and what he had only dreamed. There'd been more and more quarrelling recently. It made him furious, he felt he was being unfairly blamed for doing or not doing things that he couldn't remember any more. In the end he was almost sure that his wife and daughter were hand in glove against him, hiding things on purpose and saying he'd done this or that, just to make him look like a liar and thus infuriate him.

From the evidence of the police officer
Hermann Irgang, now retired,
eighteen years after the events concerned

Like I said, I told Zauner to sit down. He
was crouching there in silence, clutching
the shirt tightly in his hands. The liquid
ran out of it, dripped on the floor and
formed a puddle there. Half the kitchen
was already awash. I went over, took the
knotted fabric out of his hands and put it
beside the sink. The whole time, old Zauner
just sat there without moving.

Then we went over to the sofa. Afra was
lying there with her eyes closed, but there
was a gaping wound on her forehead, right
on the hairline. Her hair was reddish with
blood, and her hands were cut and scratched

as if she'd tried with all her might to defend herself. There must have been a terrible struggle between them before he overpowered her and threw her on the sofa. All the same, she looked very peaceful lying there. I'll never forget it. It was as if death had come as a release, and yet dying like that must have been so cruel for her.

Weinzierl and I both stood looking at the corpse without a word. Out in these parts folk don't get murdered, not by friends and certainly not by their own fathers. When you die, you die in your own bed, of sickness, in childbirth, of consumption, or of old age because it's simply time for you to go. Very occasionally someone dies in an accident or at work. In the woods or the fields. The only violence we see around here is a bit of brawling in the pub, or quarrelling over girls at the fair on the anniversary of the consecration of the church, when the lads throw tankards at each other's heads. But they're always dead drunk by then, can't hardly keep on their feet. It's surprising enough they can even attack each other with the tankards in that state, without losing their balance. And afterwards there's always a lot of talking, they all get worked up, they shout and accuse each other of starting the fight, and some of them begin crying like babies.

But here? Old Zauner sat on his chair and never moved, no weeping nor wailing. Me, I felt sure that if I'd been in his place, and it was my daughter lying there in her own blood, it would break my heart. I'd be pacing around the room mad with grief and pain, accusing God of making the world such a bad place and not stopping what I loved best being taken from me. But the old man just sat there as if it were nothing to do with him.

We didn't see the little boy until later. He was lying under a shawl beside the sofa, crying quietly.

I knew there was no helping Afra now. But when we found the child under the woollen shawl and he was still breathing, I hoped if I got him to the doctor right away then the little mite could be saved. So I lost no time, I put him in a basket, and I cycled off to Dr Heunisch with it as fast as I could go.

I told young Weinzierl to watch the suspect and never take his eyes off him, not for a moment, until I got back with the doctor and the murder squad.

Because when someone is murdered it's not a case for a little village policeman anymore: that's when the specialists come in.

I got in touch with our colleagues in the criminal investigation department, and about three in the afternoon I was back on the scene of the crime with the murder squad, and at four the forensics people arrived with someone from the public prosecutor's office.

The little boy died later in hospital.

Johann

He didn't know how long he'd been sitting in this room. They had taken him away with them and brought him here. When they were driving away from the house he had turned and looked out of the small rear window of the car. The washing was still hanging on the line, like an impenetrable white wall. The wind had dropped, the storm had never broken.

It must be late afternoon by now, but he had lost all sense of time. The air in the room was stuffy: in spite of the heat the window was closed and had bars outside. As far as he could tell, it looked out on a small inner court-yard. There was nothing green in sight, not a ray of sun, the view was cut off by the wall at the other side of the yard. It was greyish-brown, the plaster was coming off in many places and showing the bricks underneath. There was a small square table in the room and two chairs, nothing else. The police officers had told him that he had to wait here, so he waited patiently, still clad only in his undershirt and his work trousers.

The door opened, and a man much larger and stronger than Johann himself came in. That made him uncomfortable; he felt as if the stranger were filling the whole room, every corner of it. The man sat down on the chair opposite him and spoke calmly to Johann Zauner. He briefly introduced himself, but the old man couldn't remember the name. Then he asked Johann for his own full name, his address, the names of his wife and his daughter. But he spoke so softly that Johann had difficulty in following what he said. The stranger was trying to inject a note of familiarity into his voice, just as if they had known each other for years. Johann Zauner distrusted that kind of familiarity; he had encountered it often enough to know that it boded no good. The man opposite him noticed the old man's wariness.

Johann thought how he had come home from mowing that day; he thought of the washing blowing in the wind. Large sheets, as white as blossom. The door was open, and there was no one to be seen in the yard. The morning had been oppressively sultry, and there was an approaching thunderstorm in the air. He had hurried to get the mowing done before it began raining. On the way home from the railway embankment, dark clouds had come up in the sky. He was sweating, he had rolled up the sleeves of his shirt. He went into the shed, hung the scythe up in its place, and then he went over to the house. The enamel bucket stood by the door with the big ladle in it. He mopped the sweat from his face with his handkerchief, scooped up water in the ladle and drank it greedily. Only then did he go into the house.

A loud noise. The stranger pushed his chair aside and leaned forward. He propped himself on the table with his clenched fists, leaning forward as far as he could, coming very close to Zauner. Zauner could feel the man's breath, smell his sweat. The man's voice rose until finally he began shouting, saying he wanted to hear the truth, the whole truth, he wanted to know everything. Johann Zauner didn't know what to reply. All he could have said was that Afra was dead, and they had taken Albert away. So he said nothing, lowered his eyes and looked down at his hands, folded in his lap. They were calloused and cracked. His fingers were crooked, his joints gnarled from the hard work he had had to do all his life. On many days they hurt so much that he could hardly use them. The other man shouted at him, asking what he had done. What was he supposed to say?

He had risen early in the morning, before sunrise. He had said his morning prayers, and then he had gone into the kitchen as usual. Breakfast was already on the table. He sat down in his place opposite the crucifix on the wall, said grace, and ate. Then he had gone out to the shed, had put the whetstone in his pocket, taken the scythe and gone to the railway embankment to mow the little meadow, which belonged to him, and was just large enough to provide for the two goats and the cow. Money had always been short, and poverty was a guest seen only too often in their house, but since there had been two more mouths to feed when Afra and the child came home, it all had to stretch even further than before. However, they would manage, even though the Lord God had tried them sorely. He could have told the man all that, but he said only, 'I got up and went out to the meadow to mow it.'

Hadn't there been a quarrel that morning?

Johann Zauner couldn't remember any quarrel, only how the child lay on the floor panting for breath. He had knelt down to pick the little boy up and hold him tight. Then he had gone out to get help. The toddler had been heavy in his arms, and his stiff hands hurt.

'Did you quarrel with your daughter?' The other man repeated the question.

Johann said quietly, without going into the matter, 'My hands hurt so much.'

'Why do your hands hurt? Do they hurt because you kept hacking at your daughter and your grandson with that hoe? Is that why you're hurting?' the stranger asked, and he went on, 'Tell me, do your hands hurt because you hit them? With your hoe?'

'The hoe was lying there. I pushed it away.'

'What or whom did you push away? The hoe, your daughter's body?'

'It was lying there, the hoe was lying there.'

'Where was the hoe lying?'

The old man said nothing.

'What was the matter with Afra?'

'I couldn't tell, she was just lying there.'

'And the little boy, what about him?'

'The baby was breathing heavily.'

'The bastard, did he bother you? The child you didn't want to have there?'

'He was breathing so heavily.'

'He was always in your way, wasn't he?'

'Always getting in the way. Always underfoot. Always there.' And he went on quietly. 'It wasn't right of Afra.

Wasn't right to have the baby. But what could I have done?'

'So you hit the bastard child with the hoe, and your daughter too?'

'Hit with the hoe, yes, Afra is dead. There was blood everywhere.'

'What about the child?'

'The child was all over blood.'

'Show me your arms.'

The old man stretched out his arms.

'Why are your forearms covered in scratches?'

'It comes of the work, the scratches come of the work and then they heal up.'

He lowered his arms again.

'How can all those scratches come of the work? Isn't it a fact that you'd been fighting with your daughter? Come on, tell me, why did you do it? What wasn't right about Afra?'

'I couldn't tell, she was just lying there.'

The old man sat where he was, and from then on said no more. He only thought of Afra, and how she had been standing at the door of the house again in the summer of 1944. He had taken her in then, had simply taken her in. And when she said, later, that she was pregnant, he didn't ask any questions then, either, but he knew she had sins on her conscience, sins before God. Only later did he find out the whole truth.

He looked at his hands, and whatever else the man asked him he did not reply.

When the man put a piece of paper in front of him and told him to sign it, he signed his name. Then he put the pen down, looked at the man, and asked in a firm voice, 'Can I go now?'

'Not yet.'

Upper Palatinate Daily

Saturday, 26 July 1947

Local News

Double Murder in Finsterau

On the morning of 22 July, the Einhausen police were informed that two persons had been killed at a property in the village of Finsterau. The police immediately informed the public prosecutor's office, and called in the murder squad. At 1600 hours an investigating committee led by public prosecutor Dr Augustin went to the scene of the crime and ascertained that Afra Zauner, unmarried, aged 24 years, and her illegitimate child Albert, aged about two years, had been killed by means of blows to the head inflicted by an axe or similar instrument. Afra Zauner died at once, the child died of his injuries in hospital ten hours later.

The former railway worker Johann Zauner,
aged 59, father and grandfather respectively
of the two victims, is suspected of their murder
and was taken into custody. He has now confessed to the crime. An autopsy of the bodies
performed on Tuesday in the presence of the
investigating judge confirmed beyond any
doubt that the cause of death in both cases was
a number of heavy blows to the skull.

Just the sort of thing, thought the reporter who wrote the
story, that you might expect to happen in a place with a
name literally meaning dark meadow.

Afra

Afra picks up the basket, puts the hoe into it. She pushes the washing on the line aside with her hand and slips past the sheets. She can hear the little boy crying and hurries back to the house to see to him. She puts the basket down on the bench beside the door. Albert is already coming into the corridor inside the doorway to meet her, his face wet and smeared with tears and the snot running from his nose. She picks the little boy up and carries him into the kitchen, where she puts him down on the kitchen table, takes her handkerchief out of her apron pocket and wipes his face with it.

'Don't be scared, Albert, I'm here. I only popped outside for a minute to hang the washing on the line. I won't leave you alone.' She speaks comfortingly to him, and hugs him tightly. She feels his little body trembling with his tears.

'I'm here, darling, Mama is here, do you hear me? Did you have a bad dream?'

Slowly, the child in her arms calms down.

Afra hears a knock at the kitchen door, and next moment the door is opened and the visitor comes in. She lets go of the child and turns round.

'What are you after this time?' Afra snaps at the visitor. Albert is still standing on the table; she feels him clutching her arm with both hands.

'The door wasn't locked, so I came in. I thought I'd be welcome,' he tells her.

'My father isn't here, if it's him you want.'

'I know he isn't here, I saw him go out to mow the meadow by the railway embankment.'

'Then what do you want here, Hetsch?'

Afra can't stand him; as long as she can remember she's felt uneasy in his presence. She can't say why, he's never given her any cause for it, at least none that would account for her dislike, but she has this oppressive sense of fear when he's in the same room. It is here now, it's in the air, she can't shake it off, and he seems to feel that himself. Any other man would go away, but he likes it, it spurs him on. He's been courting her in his own way for a year; he turns up whenever there's an opportunity, he waits around for her when he thinks he'll find her on her own.

'Don't want anything, don't need anything. Just wanted to make sure everything was all right. I'll be off again if you're in a hurry,' he says with his typical pretence at friendliness, distorting his face into a smile, but all the same he makes no move to leave. Instead, he sits on the bench in the kitchen and grins at Afra.

'You can see I'm busy. You're not blind, just lame.'

She turns to the little boy and lifts him down from the table. Carefully, she places him on the floor in front of her.

'Afraid of me, are you, Afra, or why do you put your child in front of you as if he's to protect you?'

'I'm not afraid, not of anyone, and certainly not of a cripple like you.'

Yet she is holding on to the child with both hands.

'Tell you what, Afra, I noticed long ago that I'm not the sort you fancy.'

'You'll try anything, though.'

Afra lets go of Albert.

'You just don't want a fellow with a hunched back. One foot shorter than the other and something the matter with his back! But there's two sides to everything in life; they didn't want me fighting under Adolf, so that's why I survived, which is more than you can say of everyone my age.'

Afra is about to walk away from the table and over to the dresser, but he grabs her wrist and pulls her close to him, so close that she can feel his breath on her face.

'A little something like that wrong with a man has its good side and its bad side. And when it comes to the nub of the matter I'm as good as any other man, and as good as a Frenchie anyway. You needn't wait for him, you know, he won't be seen around here, that's for sure.'

'Let go of me!'

She twists and turns, wriggling out of his grasp.

'I have to see to the child and then make a mid-morning snack for my father. I don't have any time to spare now.'

'Why in such a hurry? Your father won't be home from mowing for some time yet, he's not as quick as he used to be. You can offer me a mug of coffee, why don't you? I wouldn't say no.'

Hetsch is leaning back on the bench.

'If you want a coffee then go home and make it for yourself,' Afra retorts. She turns away to go over to the dresser, but once again he moves faster than she expects, and he seizes her arm again. But now he pulls himself up by her, and so they are standing face to face. He is holding both her arms close to her body. Afra can hardly move.

'I wouldn't be a bad catch for you. I need a wife who's a good manager and won't waste money. You're tough, but I don't mind that. I like tough, bitter women. In fact, I really fancy them.'

He puts his arms round her and holds her close.

Afra tries to shake him off, bracing herself against him with all her might, but she can't get free of his grip.

'I've already told you to leave me alone.'

He tries to kiss her, and she turns her head aside.

With his mouth close to her ear, very quietly, almost inaudibly, he says, 'Hey, a wildcat like you needs a man clever enough to let her have her way. And that's me, never you fear. You're not likely to get anyone else, you know.'

Then he lets go of her.

Albert has started crying again, runs to his mother and clutches her apron, but she doesn't move from the spot. 'What do you mean?'

Hetsch stands there grinning at her. 'What do you think I mean? I mean you can think yourself lucky if I take you, because no one else will, not with your brat by the Frenchman. Who knows how many others you've had? No one knows, not with a waitress in a bar.'

This time it is Afra who goes up to him and stands with her face close to his.

'You get out of here this minute. Go away.'

At that moment they both hear a loud noise. With presence of mind, Afra says, 'That's my mother up in the bedroom under the attic, so be off with you, because she'll hear me if I call for her.'

She tries not to let her fear or the fact that she is lying show.

He thinks of saying something to her, glares at her briefly, but then goes to the door without a word. Then he turns to her once more.

'You know something, Afra? I'll get you in the end. You'll have no other option. Poor folk like your family are starvelings, and your father's getting odder all the time. You can throw me out now, but I tell you one thing: I'll be back. And then I'll show you what a real man's like. You'll be grateful when I do come back.'

Afra stands there rubbing her forearm. She is trembling all over.

'Not for the world, Hetsch, not for the world!'

'We'll see about that. You won't get rid of me so easily. I always get what I want.'

And with these words he goes out.

Afra stands in the kitchen a little longer, waiting to be sure he is out of the house, and only then does she go over to the bedroom to see what made the noise. The window of the bedroom is wide open. The wind must have blown it open, and the window frame must have hit the wardrobe and made the noise. The little earthenware vase that was standing on the far corner of the windowsill has fallen to the floor and broken into many fragments. Afra goes over to the window and bolts it shut. Albert has run after her. He is picking up the bits of the vase, curious about them.

'No, Albert, you'll hurt yourself. I'll sweep it all up later.'

She takes his hand and goes out of the house. There's no one in sight. She is still upset and trembling all over. She breathes deeply, tries to concentrate on the work she must do next. She takes the basket off the bench and goes back into the kitchen. It's time to make her father's mid-morning snack. Albert is crawling over the kitchen floor, playing with a piece of wood and chattering to himself as if nothing had happened. She bends down to him, takes the piece of wood away, and puts a crust of stale bread into his hand instead.

'There's a bit of bread, or you'll be eating that stick.'

She strokes his head and kisses his forehead.

'You get everywhere, you do; there's no taking my eyes off you for a minute.'

Tired, ponderous, she straightens up and goes out to the pantry. Dark clouds have come up outside. Afra looks

through the window at the washing hanging on the line.
She will have to bring it in before the storm breaks. At that
same moment, a gust of wind blows the pantry window
open just a crack.

Theres

Whenever she thought of that day again later it all came straight back, the uneasy feeling that came over her when she set out on her bicycle in the morning to do her errands. It wasn't as if she had any real reason to feel uneasy. Afra had been wringing out the washing in the open air, and the little boy had still been sleeping peacefully in his bed. Johann had gone out to mow the meadow beside the railway embankment. Theres wanted to hurry and be back home as soon as possible, so that Afra and her father wouldn't start quarrelling again. Over the last few weeks not a day had passed without an argument between the two of them. Sometimes it was about the child – too noisy, too spoilt. Or then again it might be Afra's refusal to go to church. From month to month the trouble between father and daughter had been getting steadily worse.

But then she had been held up; her last customer, the miller's wife, hadn't been able to make up her mind, and so in the end she cycled away from Einhausen much too late. Even from a distance she saw the washing still hanging on the line in the yard, and she knew that her presentiment had been correct.

The policeman who came out of the house and walked towards her didn't have to explain. She knew that something terrible had happened, although at that moment it wasn't clear to her that the Lord God had taken all she had away from her. She had sat down on the bench and waited. The doctor came first, and then the police officers from town. At some point the priest was there, and they had accompanied her to the priest's house. When she thought about it now it was all so blurred, so unreal. She stayed there in the presbytery for the first few days until she was better and could go home.

When she spoke to Johann for the first time since his arrest, he swore to her that he hadn't done it, and she believed him.

It was in the following weeks that rumours began going around, saying that Johann had killed Afra because he had thought she was possessed by the devil. Or that the

Frenchman, the child's father, had turned up, and since Afra wouldn't let him take the little boy away he had killed them both. Every day, it seemed to Theres, a new rumour emerged. She was at a loss, and when in the end she just didn't know what to do, she went to the police. She said it couldn't have been Johann, because he had sworn to her on all that was sacred to him that he hadn't done it. The officers were friendly but firm. They told Theres she would have to reconcile herself to the fact, hard as it was for her, that her daughter and her grandson had both been killed by her husband, and he had confessed to the crime several times to the investigating officer. If he was denying it to her, his wife, it was only because he had not entirely lost all sense of shame and couldn't bring himself to tell her the truth.

Then Theres went home, lay down in bed, and after she had cried all night she began rearranging her life. It wasn't for the first time. She had had to cope with the child Afra on her own after Johann was taken away that time in the past and placed in protective custody. She had learnt to live with the way, when he was released, he screamed in his sleep almost every night. When she couldn't bear it anymore she used to get up and go into the kitchen, where she would sit on the bench next to the crucifix and look out at the dark. Until she was finally so tired that she couldn't keep her eyes open any longer. Sometimes she still had the strength to go back to bed, but usually she slept sitting at the kitchen table.

When Albert was born, and Johann didn't want to live with the shame of it, she had been the one who held the family together. He still had his God, he wanted to force everyone to stay on the straight and narrow path, and was he supposed to have killed the two of them? He had been stubborn and strange these last few months. He had no patience with the child, and he saw only the worst in Afra, yet she found it hard to believe what people told her.

Every morning she got up, tidied the house, went to the graveyard, put flowers on the grave, and on Sunday she went to Mass. Once a month she made the long journey to see Johann in prison.

And she told anyone who asked to her face that it couldn't have been Johann, because he had sworn to her that it wasn't, by God and all that was sacred to him, and she believed him.

The Doctor

When the doctor drove up in his car the old woman was hunched on the bench beside the house. The police officer who had stayed behind with her husband had told her that she couldn't go in until his colleague was back with the murder squad. The doctor spoke to her kindly, felt her pulse and gave her an injection, and then told her to wait there, he would send a message to her neighbours and they would look after her. She couldn't go into the house until the investigating team had done their work, and that would be best for her at the moment anyway. She should think of staying with friends or relations for now, he said, at least until everything was cleared up. She sat there, looked at him and nodded.

Then he went into the kitchen. The policeman and Johann Zauner were sitting at the table. The policeman jumped up when the doctor came in and said good afternoon, but the old man sat where he was, never moving from the spot.

The next thing he noticed was the remains of a midmorning snack still on the table. A glass of water, half full, a piece of bread with a bite taken out of it, some smoked meat and cheese. The knife lay beside the plate. Later he would point this, in particular, out to the public prosecutor's office. He was to say:

'Johann Zauner was sitting beside the two bodies lying on the floor, not moving. He had made himself a snack in the middle of all that chaos, he wasn't letting anything spoil his appetite even though his grandson was lying there in his own blood, dying. He didn't care at all about the boy. Or about his daughter lying on the sofa with her skull smashed in.'

He would go on to say, in his evidence, 'Although Johann Zauner is a devout Catholic and a member of the Third Order of St Francis, he is a cold, unemotional man, for how else could he sit beside the dead bodies eating?'

The doctor had only just arrived when the murder squad's vehicles also arrived outside the house. One of the police officers told Zauner to get dressed so that he could go to the police station with them. But when he made no move to do as he was told, they took him away just as he was. They led him to the car standing outside the house.

From the evidence of the former member of
the police force Josef Weinzierl,
eighteen years after the events concerned

I'd joined the police back then, but I soon
realized it wasn't the job for me. So when
my father died suddenly of blood poisoning,
and my elder brother never came home from
prison camp in Russia, I chucked it all in
and took over the butcher's shop my father
used to keep.

I was there when the daughter and grandson
of Zauner the cottager were found dead.

And I was the one left alone for quite a
while with the old man out there.

I did look more closely at the young woman's body when Irgang had left. I was young
at the time, and inquisitive, the way you

are at that age. I wasn't scared, and the sight didn't give me the creeps. If a person's dead then they're dead. Nothing to be done about it.

I must say she was a good-looking girl, that Afra. Had a lovely face and thick dark hair, very striking. She sent the lads crazy. And you may well think that didn't suit the bigoted old man. One bastard in the family was enough for him. The way she lay there you could almost have thought she was asleep. Only you didn't want to look at her hands, they were all scratched. She must have defended herself with all her might. Her fingernails were bloody, and some of them broken off, and she had a deep cut between the thumb and forefinger of her left hand.

And the kitchen was in a right mess! Broken china all over the floor. There was a little hoe lying half under the sofa, like someone had tried to push it right under with his foot.

I told Zauner to stay put on his chair, but I didn't need to, he sat there the whole time anyway. Just staring straight ahead of him. Two or three times he said something, sounded like 'Nothing to be done now,' and 'Two birds with one stone.' What he meant by that I've no idea, because when I asked him he didn't say.

After I'd looked around a bit I sat down too, and we both waited.

There was a jug of water on the table, and two glasses. And a plate and a bread-knife as well.

When I have to wait time goes so slowly, and then I always get hungry. I've been like that since I was little. I get low blood sugar, and that brings on a headache and I can't think properly. So I always have something to eat with me. But it was outside with my bike. I knew I shouldn't really let the old man out of my sight, but I was so hungry. I couldn't stand it no more. I told Zauner to go on sitting there while I nipped out to get the bag with my sandwich from the bike. I was ever so quick, it didn't take three minutes.

When I got back in, old Zauner was gone. I said to myself, now you've gone and done it, letting a murderer get away from your very first crime scene.

I turned and went back into the corridor, but then I saw the door to the bedroom was open. He was in there. I went in on tiptoe. Very quiet like, so's he wouldn't notice me watching him. The old man was kneeling beside the bed searching in the bedside table. I looked a little, sideways, and I could see he had a purse in his hand. And a box of letters on the floor beside it. Looked like he was either going to get it all out or put it back specially. First I was surprised, then the scales kind of fell from my eyes. Hey, I says to myself, the cunning old devil, he's laying a false trail. Trying to pretend there's been a robbery with murder here.

That made me furious, so I shouted at him to go and sit down again and look sharp about it.

'You just get back on that chair,' I shouted at him, and he jumped and went back into the kitchen, not another squeak out of him. Then he stayed sitting there, he didn't dare do nothing else.

I picked up the money and the papers and gave them to our colleagues from the CID.

Then I sat down at the kitchen table with him again and unpacked my snack. I got two bites of it and then Dr Heunisch arrived. Couldn't go on eating then, what would it have looked like? Then all at once it went very fast. Almost as soon as the doctor arrived so did the CID men.

Even then I knew I wasn't going to stay on in the police, and a few months later, even before the case came to court, I chucked it all in, like I said. No one never asked about my snack, no, why would they?

Oh, I almost forgot one thing. When I was out there with my bike, old Zauner's wife arrived. I told her very sternly not to go into the house, I said she'd better sit down outside for the time being. It wouldn't be long, I said, and it wasn't. Then our CID colleagues had to tell her that her daughter was dead and her grandson too. No, she didn't get to hear of it from me, not that I can remember.

Johann

Afra had left home, and then she came back again. That was around the end of the war. He hadn't asked what brought her back, and when she told him about the baby she was going to have he still didn't say anything at first. Even if he didn't think it right that she had no father for the child. But as the months went on his anger grew and grew, and he gave vent to it. He ranted and raged. However, none of the quarrelling did any good. In time, he came to think that Afra and Theres were in league behind his back. They would laugh at him, hide things so he couldn't find them, just to work him into a white-hot fury.

It simply wasn't true. He could remember everything. All the stories from the old days. It was only sometimes he couldn't think of a thing, and that was only when he really wanted to remember it, but that was normal at a certain age. He got cross or angry only when something didn't come back to his mind at once, and Afra and Theres thought he was getting peculiar because of that.

He sat down on the plank bed, and waited, and all at once he felt sure that this time, too, they'd let him go after eight weeks.

'Yea, though I walk through the valley of the shadow of death I will fear no evil, for thou art with me, thy rod and thy staff they comfort me . . .'

**From the evidence of Detective
Superintendent Ludwig Pfleiderer,
now retired,
eighteen years after the events concerned**

Criminal Investigator Hecht took on the
case at the time. He always came down hard
on capital crimes. *Hecht* being the word for
a pike as well as a surname, we always used
to call him 'the pike in the carp pond'.
That speaks for itself.

He was a tough one — when he heard we
had a case of murder or manslaughter, he
scented blood, you couldn't get him off the
case.

He didn't want anyone else with him when
he talked to a defendant. Hecht would disappear with the man into a little cell, and

he didn't come out until he had a confession. And they all confessed to him.

I can see him before me to this day, the way he always grinned from ear to ear once he had that confession. He'd put it down on the desk in front of me and say, 'Herr Pfleiderer, Herr So-and-so has confessed.' And that was it.

His methods were successful, and a successful man is always right. No one asked about the rules and regulations, we let a few things pass in Hecht's case. It wouldn't do any more these days, but right after the war . . . We were glad of every competent colleague we could get who didn't have a cloud over him, and I'm afraid you can't ask Hecht now — he's been dead five years. A heart attack, just three weeks after he took retirement. He fell over and that was that.

Theres

Two women stand among the graves near the entrance to the graveyard. Theres almost passed them before she noticed them. Automatically, without intending to, she looked their way. The women moved even closer together, trying to hide behind the gravestones. They looked to old Theres like big black crows. She didn't need to hear their voices to know what they were whispering to each other. 'Look, her over there, that's Zauner's wife.'

'Ooh, how she slinks over the graveyard! Fancy her daring to come here on a day like this!'

'The old man killed Afra on account of that bastard child.'

'Went with a Frenchman, Afra, didn't she? And then her own father killed her. It's a sin and a shame.'

'But you never know, maybe there was more to it. Old Zauner was locked up once before, under the Nazis. Once a convict always a convict, that's what they say.'

'That story about the Frenchman, I know all about that. Heard it from my sister-in-law who married over in Polzhausen, that's where Afra worked as a waitress.'

'There's bad blood in that family.'

Theres went on, acting as if she hadn't seen the two women. Since the terrible thing happened the villagers put their heads together when they saw her coming. It wasn't the dead that you had to fear, it was the living.

They had all turned up for the funeral. The whole graveyard had been full, she had never seen so many people all at once before. They had been standing on the graves and even the graveyard wall. Everyone wanted to cast a glance at the new grave. And they had all hoped that Johann would be there as well.

'Old Zauner the murderer.'

But they hadn't let him come home for the funeral, which was just as well. He wouldn't have understood, just as he didn't understand so much else going on around him recently. Every day she went to the graveyard, and she went to church on Sunday, and once a month they let her visit Johann. Every time she saw him she was more frightened than ever; he was only a shadow of his former self. He often didn't even recognize her now when she visited him. And when Theres began talking about Afra and the child, it seemed to her that he didn't know who she meant. To her, that state of mind was intolerable, for it meant taking her daughter and her grandson away from her for a second time.

Zauner's wife pushed the watering can down into the water in the stone trough with both hands. She watched air bubbles rise from the inside of the can. At first she had meant to stay away from the procession on All Saints' Day, but then she had gone after all. She had waited right at the back, and hadn't gone to stand by the grave until the last people had left after the procession round the churchyard.

She took the heavy watering can out of the water and went back along the rows of graves to Afra's. The gravel crunched at every step she took. She put the can down beside the grave, broke off the faded stems of the flowers, put them aside and watered the rest. Then she filled the font with holy water. She put her hand in her jacket pocket and was going to take out the candle to be lit for Afra's soul, when she heard a voice.

'Giving them a drink to moderate the torments of pur-
gatory, are you?'

Theres turned. Hetsch was standing behind her.

'Oh, you gave me such a fright! What are you doing,
still here? The procession is over. Why aren't you at the
inn with the others?'

Theres took the candle out of her pocket.

'Maybe there's something driving me on? Like those
poor souls supposed to walk over the graves tonight?'

'What do you mean by that?' The old woman gave him
an enquiring look.

'Didn't you ever hear about it, Frau Zauner? Tonight,
folk can see who the dead will come to take away next
year. Or maybe it's just a guilty conscience keeps me on
the move, same as you. You did see me out there on the
day it happened, didn't you?'

'I didn't see anyone. I was out and about all day.'

Theres was about to turn away, but Hetsch had a firm
hold on her arm.

'But you were there, at least you were there first thing,
I heard the noise.'

'No such thing. I was in Einhausen, Hetsch. Or that
terrible thing would never have happened.'

Hetsch let go of her and stood there, his fingers fum-
bling with his jacket. He was looking past her at the

gravestone, and suddenly he looked small and thin, although she didn't even come up to his shoulder. All the assertiveness he liked to show was gone.

'I always liked seeing Afra, and that day I wanted to know. I wanted to know if she'd bend or break. I thought I'd stay until she said yes, but then it all turned out differently and I went away.'

'If you saw anything, Hetsch, you must tell the police.'

Hetsch straightened up. It was as if a different man were suddenly standing in front of her.

'I didn't see anything. But I wanted to tell you I really did like Afra a lot. I honestly did.'

Then he turned and walked away. Theres stood there watching him go until his figure was lost in the twilight. Finally she took out her matches and lit the candle she was holding.

I shouldn't have gone out that day, she thought. He's right, it's my guilty conscience drives me here. I place the eternal light here for you so that the little one won't be afraid in the night. When you needed me, Afra, I wasn't there.

When Theres walked back to the churchyard gate past the rows of graves, it was dark, and only the lights burning on the graves lit the churchyard up a little.

She thought of what Hetsch had said about the dead, and how they would come looking for the one who was to follow them in the coming year. But the only person Theres saw walking over the graves that evening had been Hetsch himself. She made the sign of the cross.

'God have mercy on his soul.'

**From the evidence of the police officer
Hermann Irgang, now retired,
eighteen years after the events concerned**

There's something else I'd like to say here. Our investigations at the time weren't confined to Johann Zauner as the possible murderer. We kept our eyes open, we looked in all directions, even though the father had behaved very strangely from the first.

The war was only two years ago, so there were all kinds of odd characters drifting about. Many people came out from the city wanting to barter something: clothes and pictures in exchange for butter, eggs and sausage. Now and then there were some who might have frightened you, they were going around in such a ragged state. Of course we looked carefully at that sort, because we'd heard that there were two young journeymen roaming the countryside at that time. And when some people said they'd also been seen on Zauner's farm, of course we pricked up our ears, and we did all we could to find them.

At the time it wasn't so easy to find an itinerant. In addition, we didn't have names, just the fact that they were two young fellows and they'd been sleeping in a hay barn the night before the murder.

I couldn't have sworn to it that we were really going to find them, but we did manage to get on their trail.

Unfortunately it soon turned out that we'd gone to all that trouble for nothing, because they weren't able to give us any information. They did make statements saying they'd passed the house, but with the best will in the world they couldn't say whether it had been that particular day or a day or so earlier. And they couldn't tell us anything else that might have helped with our inquiries.

I don't remember now who it was that questioned them, it ought really to be in the files, but once everyone knew old Zauner had confessed the records probably weren't written up. People weren't as particular about such things then as they are today.

The suspect had confessed, and the young fellows couldn't tell us anything useful about the crime, so we just let them go again. What else could we have done? There wouldn't have been any point in questioning them again, we had no legal handle against them, and if a man hasn't seen anything then he hasn't seen anything, and no amount of questions are going to change that.

At the time the news that Zauner had confessed was going around like wildfire, but even without a confession everything pointed to him from the start. It wasn't just the endless quarrels with his daughter, his odd behaviour — he had scratches on his arms that he couldn't explain to us, as his family doctor said at the time. I can't say whether he was also examined by a doctor from the courts. We really didn't take the easy way out; in the end he was the only possible murderer.

Dr Augustin

'So what titbits have been coming your way?'

Dr Augustin drew the stack of cards from the middle of the table towards him to deal new cards to his fellow players.

'I'll tell you, never fear. Maybe it was Max? He took a critical attitude, anyway.'

Josef Loibl, sitting opposite him, grinned mischievously at Augustin.

'You two can't beat us now, you're all tensed up!'

Then he called over Augustin's head to the waitress at the bar. 'Bring me another half, Roswitha, with a beer-warmer if you have one around.' And turning to the rest of the card players, he added, 'Believe it or not, cold beer gives me heartburn. Specially when I drink it before lunch.'

'Ah, you're one of the delicate sort, can't even digest a proper beer in the middle of the morning.'

Dr Augustin had dealt the cards. He picked up his own hand and arranged the cards in it.

'Augustin, pull yourself together or I'm not playing cards with you any more. Public prosecutor or not, sometimes you're a real know-it-all,' replied the man he had addressed, and then, in a conciliatory tone, 'But seeing I'm not that way myself, would you like to bid? Then I'll say what's trumps.'

Roswitha Haimerl brought the half that Loibl had asked for, exchanged the full glass for his empty one, and made her mark on the beer mat.

'Any of the rest of you gentlemen like something to drink? Then I won't have to keep scurrying back and forth.'

'Hey, you're in a bad mood today, Roswitha. Never mind, can you bring me a lager, and I like mine cold,' replied one of the other card players, his eyes twinkling at her.

'You expect a body not to be cross if she has to keep running around for every half litre?'

Roswitha Haimerl turned and went over to the bar.

'I'll bid if you like. Makes no difference to me, you two are going to lose anyway. I'll bid seven,' said Dr Augustin.

'Seven, our public prosecutor's putting out an emergency call. Then I'll say hearts. Seven of hearts.'

This time the landlord, Hermann Müller, brought the beer to the table himself. He exchanged the glasses, put the used one on the free table beside the card players, and stood watching until the end of the trick, then took a vacant chair and sat down with the players, who were dividing the winnings between them. Coins of small denominations were pushed over the table, and the cards gathered into a pack again. Josef Loibl, who seemed dissatisfied with his share of the winnings, said, 'Come to think of it, this is an illegal game of chance, right?'

Dr Augustin, to whom the question was obviously directed, tipped the coins from the little mat into his purse and replied, 'First, playing cards and the Bavarian game of *Watten* in particular is no fun without a stake, and second, I'm not on duty. And so long as we're only playing for small change no one can be cheated. Even an old miser like you can join in, Loibl.'

Then he put his purse in his back pocket, picked up his glass and drank, saying, 'Cheers, gentlemen!'

One of the card players rose from the table, tapped it lightly with his fist, and said, 'Well, I'm off now. First I'll take a pee, then I'll go home. Food's probably on the table already in our house – and if I don't turn up I'll be in trouble. Goodbye, all, see you next Saturday.'

'Wait, I'll go with you to take a pee, and I have to go home too.'

Joseph Loibl also rose from the table.

Hermann Müller drew his chair a little closer to Dr Augustin. He put his hand in the breast pocket of his shirt, and produced a folded press cutting. He carefully smoothed it out and placed it in the middle of the table.

'Here, Augustin, something for you. Someone lost this in here yesterday. Take a good look, that's you in the photograph.'

Dr Augustin took the yellowed piece of paper and studied it attentively. 'Where did you get this? All that was ages ago.'

'Like I said, there was a guest here yesterday took a lot of drink on board, and he left the cutting here, along with his wallet and a twenty-mark note.'

The landlord searched his trouser pocket and put the wallet on the table as well.

'He was a strange sort. At first he was calm, and then he suddenly started talking all confused stuff. He knew about a murder, he said, and the man who did it was still walking about free. I thought he was a nutcase, but first thing this morning Roswitha found the wallet. When I looked at the photo I could hardly believe my eyes. I thought that was you, Augustin, half hidden at the back there, was I right?'

'Yes, that's me. And you'll laugh, I can still remember, it was my first case in court right after the assessors' examination qualifying me. It was pretty much of an open-and-shut case. But I'd be interested to hear what your guest yesterday had to say.'

So Hermann Müller told him about the incident, and Dr Augustin listened carefully. After that Augustin sat there a little longer. He had become unusually thoughtful. He finished his beer and went home.

He behaved differently from usual for the rest of the day as well. He normally went home on Saturday after his mid-morning beer, sat down at the dining table, ate lunch and then went into the living room with the newspaper. There he sat on the sofa, read the paper with close attention, and then, well pleased with himself and the world, he lay down for a little nap. But that day he left his lunch getting cold on the table and went straight to his study. He searched the shelves for old files; when he couldn't find what he was looking for, he paced restlessly around the room. Finally he left his study at home, put on his jacket, and drove to his office. He sat there until late in the evening, poring over old papers.

On Monday morning he told his colleagues that they ought to reopen the case.

Johann

The young police officer was shifting restlessly back and forth on the kitchen chair. Johann could tell, just from looking at him, how uneasy he felt in uniform. Beads of sweat were standing out on his forehead. Now and then he mopped his face dry with a handkerchief. Then he suddenly jumped up, saying he must go out for a moment to take a pee, and he, Johann, was to stay sitting there and not do anything stupid, because even if he had to go outside just briefly he'd still be keeping an eye on him.

At first the old man stayed on his chair and waited, just as the policeman had told him to do. But then his eye fell on Afra, who was still lying on the sofa. Her clothes were soaked red with blood. What was he to tell Theres when she came back? The woman who laid out the dead must come and wash Afra. There was so much to be done: the church, the funeral. What would become of Albert? He had to do something, he couldn't stay on that chair letting time run away. Theres wouldn't understand it if he only sat there doing nothing.

The old man rose from his chair. He had come to a decision, he would go over to the bedroom and fetch clean clothes for his daughter. When they laid her in the coffin she ought to be properly dressed. No one in the village must be able to say he'd let her go without her Sunday best on.

He would get the dark blue dress, the one with the lace collar, and a pair of clean stockings. He would get everything ready for the woman who came to lay Afra out. So that she could wash her and dress her neatly. He must find her rosary and prayer book, and cover up the mirror.

Theres was much better at these things, but he couldn't wait. They might come and take his daughter away any moment now. He must have everything ready.

Johann Zauner went out of the kitchen, across the corridor and into the bedroom. It wasn't as tidy in there as Afra usually left it. The wardrobe stood a little way open, some of her underclothes were hanging out of the drawers or lying scattered on the floor. He bent down, picked them up and tried to put them back as best he could into the wardrobe. As he closed its door he took a step sideways and came up against the bedside table. A shoebox that he hadn't seen there before fell off it and hit the floor. All Afra's possessions lay scattered round him. Letters, buttons, hairpins and her rosary, even the prayer book lay there open.

Johann Zauner knelt down on the floor awkwardly, picked up first the mourning pictures that had fallen out of the *Order of Divine Service* and put them and the prayer book back on the bedside table, where the prayer book belonged. So did the rosary. He would have to take them both into the kitchen with him. Then he tidied up the letters as well as he could, and put them back in the shoebox. He bent down to look for the buttons, and under the bedside table he found a banknote and several coins. He picked them up from the floor, straightened up, still on his knees, and took his wallet out of the back pocket of his trousers; they would need every penny they could scrape together for the funeral.

'What are you doing here? Get right back to your chair in the kitchen!'

Johann Zauner turned to the door in alarm. The young policeman was standing in the doorway, his face bright red, shouting at him. Johann got to his feet, with difficulty, supporting himself on the bed with his elbow. Confused, he held out the hand in which he was still holding the money he had picked up. The policeman was beside him in an instant, tearing the banknote from him and getting him to hand over the coins too.

'This stays with me. Disposing of the evidence – that won't do. It's against the law. Why did you do that, Zauner? I suppose you were planning to make it look like robbery with violence, but I'm here, see? Mind you get back into the kitchen, and don't you touch anything else in here. And you'd better give me that wallet.'

Johann Zauner apologized humbly and did as he was asked. He left the prayer book and rosary lying on the bedside table.

From the statement of
public prosecutor Dr Augustin,
eighteen years after the events concerned

I was a very young public prosecutor at the
time, full of enthusiasm for my profession,
and convinced that I was making an important contribution to the construction of a
just legal system with a clean record. I
was idealistic and a little naive, as one
can be only in one's youthful years.

Accordingly, the Zauner case still lin-
gers in my memory, even after such a long
interval of time. However, for safety's
sake I have called up the old files and
reread them. Here I would like to summarize
the image we had formed at the time of our
investigation.

The old records show that when we were first faced with the crime, Johann Zauner made an entirely indifferent and apathetic impression. He did not seem to be in the least moved by the tragedy, at least to outward appearance. According to one witness statement in the files, he even made himself a mid-morning snack soon after committing the murder. He also made stupid and primitive attempts to pretend that the situation was one of robbery with violence, by scattering money and other small possessions of the dead girl around her room. When the absurdity of this act, which took place in the presence of a police officer and after the first police investigation, was pointed out to him, he initially apologized at length and said he would tidy it all up again.

Herr Zauner was questioned on various occasions in the course of the investigation. His few explanations of the act matched the clues that had been found. At the time of the investigation we never had the least doubt of his guilt. In addition, he confessed to the murder in front of an officer. A confession weighs a great deal in court, it crowns the evidence as the clearest and pre-eminent means of proof. While the investigation was in progress he never retracted his statement, nor did he offer mitigating circumstances, and not just once but several times he was offered an opportunity to distance himself from it. True, it is a drawback that he said nothing clearly about his motive, but given the very simple structure of his personality that is not necessarily surprising. He said he had been furious, and indeed, literally, that he had been 'in a murderous mood', repeating several times that in that state he did not know what he was doing. Asked why he also killed the child, he said that the little boy, as he put it, 'was always getting underfoot', and that it had been 'all linked together'.

Even when he was first questioned, his ponderous manner and mental lethargy were noticeable. Consequently, Zauner was sent to a psychiatric institution. The findings of the investigation were before the court at the time.

It all seemed perfectly clear, and most important of all the defendant had confessed. There is no getting around a confession. It may be that the confession is a highly simplified view of what happened, but confession by the defendant is an act of mental cleansing comparable to spiritual cleansing by confession to a priest. The guilty man, like the sinner, acknowledges his guilt and thus achieves relief and peace of mind. Or so at least we were taught when I was studying.

As I said, I was still at the beginning of my career, but many years have passed since then, and I have learnt to question many things. I have learnt that there can be very different reasons for confessing to a crime, and the person concerned may sometimes confess fervently and very convincingly even when he never committed that crime at all. It can be difficult to recognize the truth, and sometimes even conscientious police officers hear only what

they would like to hear; in that, they are
no different from all the rest of humanity.
What was ultimately left was the fact of
Johann Zauner's confession. And so proceedings were brought against him.

Towards the end of the trial, when all
the witnesses had made their statements and
all the expert opinions had been heard,
there was a sudden change. All at once
Zauner rose to his feet and retracted his
confession. Suddenly he might have been
a different man. He proved obstinate and
refractory. He denied what he had said,
showing not the least understanding of it.
There were tumultuous scenes in the court-
room when he 'called God to witness' that
he had not committed the murder. The pre-
siding judge threatened to clear the court
if those present did not calm down. Not
one of them believed a word the defendant
said. Johann Zauner shouted that he was not
guilty. The judge tried again and again to
induce him to relieve his conscience by
repeating his confession. However, Zauner
was obstinate, and even offered to make a

statutory declaration swearing to his inno-
cence, being unaware that he could not call
for such a declaration. Even counsel for
the defence was unable to pacify him. I
would be lying if I were to say that at the
time I was not entirely convinced of his
guilt. Johann Zauner was convicted on the
grounds of a heavy weight of proof and the
statements of countless witnesses. But as
in all trials depending on circumstantial
evidence, there is always a lingering rem-
nant of uncertainty.

I do not know whether today I would still
call, as I did eighteen years ago, for a
prison sentence of eight years in a peni-
tentiary for each of the two murders, and
with judicial approval for a total prison
sentence of twelve years.

The court finally decided on sentencing
him to ten years in prison, and subsequent
preventive detention. It was stipulated
that after he had served his sentence he
should be confined in a psychiatric institution on account of his mental deficiencies
and the resulting danger of his reoffending.

The medical experts had decided that Zauner's derangement meant he was not entirely responsible for his actions.

I was satisfied with this decision of the court. We had no other option, in view of the findings of our investigations, and the sentence was correct in law; whether it was just is another question.

No court in the world can do perfect justice, we can only come to our decisions in line with the evidence available at the time of the trial, and of course in the context of the legal possibilities. Unfortunately, we are too often wrong in our interpretation of the truth, or from where we stand we see only a small part of the whole. Truth is a shy child, and its mother, justice, is usually depicted as blind.

Matthias Karrer

At some time in the night he woke up. It was dark, and he was alone in the bar of the inn. Even the landlord had left. He must have dropped off to sleep; the beer mat and his bill were still on the table. His arm hurt because it had been lying at an awkward angle. In fact he hurt right up to his shoulders, his whole body had seized up. His hand had gone to sleep, and he had to massage it for a while with the other hand before he could use it again. At first he couldn't remember where he was when he woke up, or what he was doing here. But then it came back to him. He'd stayed on here in the Baitz area yesterday evening. At first he came into the inn only to buy something to eat. Out and about all day, going from house to house. Ringing bells. Towards seven he'd had enough of it, he'd thought he deserved his hard-earned supper.

Sharpening knives didn't bring in much money these days. People didn't value his craft any more. Even ten years ago he'd made a decent living, but now? People these days bought mass-made implements, knives with plastic handles, available for the price of a sandwich. All cheap, all easy to come by; if you needed something new you went to Woolworth's, where they sold their customers rubbish. You couldn't sharpen a knife like that, its blade would bend the moment you so much as looked at it, and if he put it on the whetstone he could expect it to break, it was such poor quality.

'The good old days are over,' he said to himself under his breath, holding on to the table to help him get to his feet. He'd been on the road as long as he could remember. He wasn't a gypsy; his family belonged to the continental travelling people known as the Yenish. They had been pedlars, knife-grinders and basket-weavers for generations, all of them decent folk with a licence to trade on the road and a small house in the Unterlichtenwald area. In the bad times of the Third Reich, when even the licence to trade wasn't valid any more and his father had been forced to go and work in the munitions factory, that little house had saved their lives, even if the other Yenish looked down on them for having a fixed address.

'If you live in a house you're not a Yenish any more, you're one of the Gachi people.'

But the fact was that without a fixed address they'd all have been bound for Dachau.

A man like Karrer couldn't stay in one place, and after the war he was off again. It's in your blood, you can't change that, he told himself.

Two or three times a year he came to these parts, so he knew the inn. He had his usual routes. It was two years after the war he'd been here for the first time, and after that every year apart from a few interruptions.

'Damn it all, that's long ago!' he said to himself under his breath, and getting unsteadily to his feet he patted his jacket in search of cigarettes and his lighter. However, as he couldn't find either he sat down on the chair again.

He'd been in Einhausen again yesterday, so he'd come in here. He had ordered brawn. As usual. They made the best brawn in the whole region here in the Baitz area. The waitress had a sharp tongue, but the food was good and you got value for your money.

A couple of guests at the next table had started talking politics. He listened for a while, and then joined in their dispute over the table, until finally he picked up his beer and sat down with them.

Later, when the room was emptying, the talk became more and more heated. Stories from the 'old times' went back and forth, and comments on how with someone like Adolf in charge, this or that wouldn't happen.

He hadn't noticed how much he had drunk. Normally he was moderate in his drinking, but yesterday . . . well, he must have had a few too many beers with schnapps as chasers.

Once again, he searched his pockets in vain for a cigarette.

'Damn it, where the hell did I put them?'

If the others hadn't left, he would have gone on arguing and drinking, and that on a day when business had been slow. When the last at his table got tired of the dispute and went home, he had ordered a final half of beer and a snifter of fruit spirits as a chaser.

'No point in standing on one leg.'

And as always when he'd been drinking, and was discontented with the stupidity and injustice of the world, the whole wretched story came back into his mind. What still annoyed him was that they'd never caught the real murderer. Worse, they hadn't even looked for him. The man who'd fucked the young woman back then and was probably leading a merry life now, maybe with a wife and child. The man who certainly didn't have to toil like him day after day; could be he had a good, secure income. While he, Matthias? He'd never really done anything very bad, and yet it was downhill all the way with him. To this lot he was only a knife-grinder, a good-for-nothing, a gypsy, and who bothered to know that he'd usually tried to be honest?

They just won't let you get anywhere, he said to himself.

Still dazed with alcohol, he tried getting up from the chair again. Finally he was standing on both feet, although his legs were still shaky. Slowly and carefully, he felt his way in the dark over to the door. It was bolted. From there he made his way to the bench under the window.

On many days it would simply have been better to stay in bed in the morning and not get up at all, and yesterday had been one of those days. Everything had gone wrong from the morning onwards, even as he was still on the way from Einhausen to Finsterau. Some bastard had left a board with nails in it lying in the road. He hadn't seen it and had driven his Lloyd 600 over it. Result, a flat tyre. After he had changed the wheel and looked around him, slowly smoking a cigarette, he had noticed it. He and his car were at the very place in Finsterau where the road forked, and if you took one way you reached the place where the young woman had been murdered not long after the war.

He opened the window.

He ought to have turned back there and then. Such places were never good news. It hadn't been a coincidence: it couldn't have been.

She's still haunting the place, he thought. Out there the poor soul can't find peace. No wonder I got a flat tyre at that very place yesterday. Oh, Lord God and all the holy sacraments, now my jacket's caught on something.

He tried at length to get his jacket free. He pulled and tugged, and as he did so the cigarettes and lighter he'd been looking for fell out onto the windowsill. He picked up both and scrambled through the window frame into the open air, where he lit himself a cigarette and inhaled the smoke deeply. He had a stale taste in his mouth, and his throat was sore.

God, he thought, what a thirst I have. Even tobacco tastes bad.

He flicked the cigarette away, and left.

Theres

'Johann's lawyer called the priest. He said I was to tell you it's urgent, and could you come over here to the telephone? He said he'd ring again in an hour's time.'

The priest's housekeeper was still out of breath as she stood at the door. Theres took off her overall, got her jacket, slipped into the shoes standing ready and hurried over to the presbytery with the housekeeper.

Over the phone, the defence lawyer told her that they had moved Johann from prison and sent him to the mental hospital. It was better for him that way, said the lawyer. He had been going downhill more and more with every passing day, until finally the doctor in the prison infirmary said he couldn't be responsible for the outcome if he stayed there any longer.

'This is a prison, not a madhouse,' he had said. The infirmary simply was not designed for cases like Johann, which made his stay there unreasonable both for Johann himself and for his fellow prisoners. The doctor had spoken to the public prosecutor and the judge, and all three had already had their doubts about Johann and whether he was right in the head. In all the conversations they'd held with him they hadn't come a step closer to the actual course of events during the crime. For him personally, as his defence counsel, said the lawyer, that meant that the case had never been easy. After further discussion they had come to the conclusion that no one with all his wits about him could murder his daughter and grandson in such a barbaric manner. And in all the weeks and months that had now passed only a madman would never show remorse. Even with an ice-cold murderer, sooner or later a motive would be seen, and then the case could be explained.

'Believe me, Frau Zauner, transferring him to a mental hospital will surely be easier for him to bear in his present state of mind than staying in prison. There can be no question of reopening proceedings; no new evidence has turned up. I'm very sorry, but that's all I can still do for you.'

And with that he hung up.

Theres stood there for a moment longer, and then she

put the receiver back on its stand. All she said to the house-keeper, who was looking at her enquiringly and curiously, was, 'They've taken him to the Carthusian hospital.'

Then she left.

It had begun drizzling outside. Theres took no notice of the rain. It began raining harder and harder, but that made no difference to her. She finally got home drenched to the skin.

Two days later the official letter came. It said where exactly Johann had been taken, and that now he wasn't in prison but in the closed section of the psychiatric hospital she would be able to visit him more often if she liked. The very next week she went to see him and stayed as long as the doctors would let her.

Johann

In the hospital there were four or six of them to a room, in contrast to his prison cell. The light never went entirely out even by night; there was dim illumination all the time. As soon as it got dark outside the barred windows he became restless. He couldn't stay in his bed; he walked around or sat very close to the other patients and stared at them. If he was taken back to his own bed by the nursing staff and tied to the bedstead by his arms and legs, to keep him from wandering around again, he began screaming. Usually he calmed down after a while; sometimes, when he didn't, he was taken out of the room and brought back next morning, still upset and exhausted by the night he had passed.

He spent his days sitting on his bed in the room or

walking up and down the long corridor, hour after hour. At first he counted his footsteps, counted the number of times he went along the corridor, but gradually he forgot the numbers. Other wretched figures like him sat in the whitewashed corridors. Sometimes he babbled to himself, screamed or wept. Every mood could change to the next within a second. He was living in his own little world, separated from everyone else, incapable of speaking to the others or showing interest in anyone – like the toothless old woman who always waited for him to pass her room. Then she would hurry towards him, grab his face, try to get her fingers in his mouth, his nostrils. She was not to be shaken off, she thrust her dry forefingers into his eyes. He defended himself as well as he could, shouted for help until the male nurses came and took the old woman away.

On many days he could not bear to feel his shirt next to his skin. However often the male nurses tried to dress him he tore it off. If they tied his hands behind his back he rolled on the floor, trying to get an end of the fabric in his teeth so as to pull it away, get rid of it, like a lizard shedding its old, dry skin.

In the rooms with doors on the other side of the corridor patients sat disentangling wool for hours on end. If they had freed a strand of any length from the bundle, they would tie it to the other strands and roll them up into brightly coloured balls.

The doctor told him to join in the work in this room, and Johann, who wasn't used to being indoors all day, obeyed, sat with the others and disentangled woollen threads.

In time, he saw only a fragmentary view of all around him. The days were like each other, broken only by visits from the doctors. The one thing he noticed was that his thoughts were wandering more and more, and even his faith was no comfort to him. He tried to resist the loss of it, he wanted to write down his tormenting thoughts to be rid of them, but his hands would no longer obey him, so he began to put his memories into empty bottles, filling them to the brim with words and then carefully closing them. If he held the bottles to his ear, he thought he could hear his own voice inside. When he opened a bottle the words slipped out again. But the nurses and doctors didn't understand what he was doing, and thought him totally deranged now. Yet how else could he have protected his memories? He had to shut them away before they were lost for ever, for he seemed to forget more with every sentence he spoke. And they never stopped tormenting him here, always asking him the same thing over and over again, until finally all that was left of him was an empty husk.

Afra

Afra closes the window and bolts it firmly down. She shakes it again once, then takes the preserved sausage that hangs in the pantry, cuts another piece off the smoked meat, puts it all in her apron and goes into the kitchen.

Meanwhile, Albert has got up and gone over to the cubbyhole in the kitchen, leaving the crust of bread in the middle of the room. Afra puts the meat and sausage on a wooden platter, places it on the table with a jug of water and two glasses. She bends down, picks up the bread from the floor and puts it back in Albert's hand.

'There, dear, you'll need good teeth, but don't chew on that piece of wood, you'd better leave it alone or you'll hurt yourself.'

Afra tries to make her voice sound cheerful; she doesn't want to show that she is still worn out by her argument with Hetsch. How does he manage to pester her so much? He must have passed her father – if he were in the house Hetsch would have had to hold back. Always keeping up appearances. So she's a tavern girl, is she, available to all comers?

'Oh, leave me alone, you lying lot!' she mutters to herself.

Albert looks enquiringly at his mother.

'Not you, darling, I didn't mean you.'

Afra picks Albert up in her arms. He is holding the hard crust of bread in both hands, chewing it.

'There you are, something nice to suck.'

She bends her head and kisses him on the forehead.

When there is a knock at the door, she is afraid for a split second that Hetsch has come back. She holds the child more tightly, as if she could shield him from some misfortune, and then opens the door. In the doorway stands one of the two journeymen who have been roaming the countryside.

'The door wasn't locked, so I came right in. Just wanted to ask if we could wash out there at the well? And maybe you'd have a mug of milk or a bite to eat? A crust of bread would do for us.'

'I can give you some curds, and a slice of bread. I'll bring it out to you.'

'May God repay you.'

'Where are the two of you off to, then?'

'Everywhere and nowhere.'

'That's no kind of destination. Meanwhile, you can go back to your friend, I'll bring the curds and bread out to you.'

Afra turns away, still with the child in her arms. Albert has put the hand holding his gnawed crust of bread round her neck, and he is clinging to her collar with his other hand. However, the stranger stays where he is, making no move to go. The child pulls gently at his mother's earlobe. She turns.

'I said I'll bring it out. No need for you to stand around the kitchen.'

Afra looks distrustfully at the stranger. Until Albert begins whining and struggling, and attracts all her attention to himself. He writhes in her arms, wanting her to put him down on the floor.

'And maybe you'd have a little mug of warm water for shaving?'

'Yes, if that's all.'

Afra puts Albert down and goes over to the kitchen

stove. She opens the lid of the hot water compartment and scoops some out into a small mug.

'Did you two find a place to sleep last night?' She hands the young man the water. 'This'll have to do. I haven't quite filled it, so you can add a little cold. Got everything else you need? A mirror, or shall I get you my father's?'

'We don't need a mirror, but thanks all the same. I'll bring your mug right back.'

'No hurry. When I'm finished in here I'll bring the breakfast out to you. I have to go into the yard, there's washing still hanging on the line, and it looks like the weather won't hold for long.'

The young man is still standing in the same spot, now with the can of water in his hands, not moving. Afra is unsure of herself, doesn't know what to do. To persuade the visitor to leave, she goes over to the window and looks out.

'It won't break just yet. I don't think it'll rain in a hurry,' she hears him say. He waits a moment longer, holding the can of water, as if he would like to add something more, but then turns and goes over to the door.

Afra, who has turned her back to him, hears him close the door behind him.

'That fellow didn't know what he wanted, did he, Albert? As pushy as Hetsch.' And then, 'Oh, my word,

Albert, I have to sweep up the little broken vase still lying on the bedroom floor. Wait here and Mama will soon be back, all right? I'll just get the dustpan and brush and go over there. I won't be long, and stay away from the stove, Albert, or you'll burn your fingers.'

But Albert wasn't listening to her; he was sitting on the floor playing with his bit of bread, making little pellets of bread dough mixed with his spit and rolling them back and forth.

From the statement of
Matthias Karrer, pedlar and knife-grinder,
eighteen years after the events concerned

Right after the war I left the Unterlichtenwald area. Under the Nazis my father hadn't
been allowed to go around with his licence
trading from door to door. He was always
telling me what that free way of life was
like. My folk have always been on the
road, it's part of us, like air is part
of breathing; it's in our blood. My father
came into the world beside the family's
caravan, on the road, just like that. Same
as his father before him and all our ances-
tors before that. Our folk went on the road
with horse-drawn caravans, with bag and
baggage, ducks, geese, pigs, everything, all

their household goods. We had our usual places and we went there. Everyone knew when we was coming. We was honest folk, not gypsies, we were Yenish.

Must have been the spring of '47 when I set out. I packed my rucksack and left. The first Karrer to go off on his own, not with the whole tribe, but I knew I'd always find some of us on the road. And so I did. Our folk know each other by their talk, it's a mixture of cant and Bavarian and Yiddish; in fact a bit of everything, just like us.

So then I met two fellows in autumn that year, Otto and Wackes. I don't know what the right name of Wackes was. He was just called that because Wackes is our word for a Frenchman. He was always saying he'd make his way through to the French and join the Legion. That's the kind of fellow Wackes was.

I let the pair of them persuade me to do a few silly things, nicking something here, walking off with something else there. But at that age things look different, and you want to impress your new friends. When you're young you're stupid too. It don't do in the long run.

And in Alling, Otto and I got caught climbing into the bakery. We'd had nothing much to eat the day before, only a few apples still almost green and a crust of stale bread. All that time I was kind of confused, what with hunger and the air inside my belly going to my head.

It was just dark when we came to the village. All day Wackes wouldn't leave us in peace. He said how simple it was to climb into the baker's shop, and he knew his way around it 'like he knew his own waistcoat pocket'. He'd been put to work there in the war, and he still had accounts to settle from those days. The baker had been a real slave-driver, and it wouldn't hurt if he had to pay for that a little now. And he'd do it himself, said Wackes, if we didn't dare, but his hand hurt and wouldn't heal. So as I'd believe him, he stretched it out to me, and I could see that he had a deep cut over the ball of his hand, with the skin gaping open and the flesh standing proud.

'What's more,' he said to me, 'it means you can show if there's really anything to you, or if you're just talking hot air while you shit your pants. We can do without a mate like that, eh, Otto?'

Otto nodded as if he agreed. As a young lad you don't wait to be asked twice, so it was agreed. We'd nick money and bread or whatever else we could find.

The Frenchman was to be on watch in front, and Otto and I would get into the bakehouse through the back window.

The baker had his bedroom right above the bakehouse. Wackes hadn't told us that. Maybe he didn't know. And when I'd broke the window next to the door it must have woken them upstairs. It made such a noise, the breaking glass would have woken the dead. The window was gone and we climbed into the bakehouse. And then it all went very fast. We didn't even have time to look for money or anything else. The baker took us by surprise. If there's someone holding a shotgun under your nose then you know it's time to keep still. Before we'd even looked around, the police were there and taking us away. That bastard Wackes was gone. So it was only Otto and me ended up in clink.

Hetsch

The conversation with Afra had not gone at all well. Hetsch was marching through the wood, angrily complaining to himself. He was annoyed: why wouldn't she take him? She'd gone with that Frenchman, hadn't she? Was it just because of his short legs? He had one of the largest farms in the village, a woman like Afra could think herself lucky: in the usual way she'd never make such a good catch. But it was his own fault, he'd gone about it the wrong way. However, with every step his resentment grew. Who and what did she think she was? A Frenchman's floozy! A girl with nothing to her name, and with a child into the bargain. If she was going to be the single mother of a bastard, it ought at least to be a local bastard. But in this case? Afra was nothing but a tart. A cheap woman of easy virtue. And he'd been stupid enough to let himself be intimidated. He'd listened to her talking big, and he'd run away like a little schoolboy. Because he was shit-scared of Zauner's wife. He was a fool, an idiot. Not that he'd even seen Theres. And if he had, so what? What could she have against it? They were paupers, miserable little cottagers, they should be glad he wanted to take Afra, bastard and all. Theres would have one worry less. Anyone could see how badly off they were.

Hetsch hurried on through the wood. The air was oppressive, sweat was running down his back. From time to time he mopped his forehead dry with his handkerchief. He ought to have tackled the thing differently, quite differently. Next time he wouldn't let himself be sent off like that. He'd do the job properly. But who knew when there'd be another such opportunity, and when he'd pluck up his courage again? It could be a long time yet, so why wait? He'd go back, now. It couldn't be postponed, he wanted to know now. Now, on the spot.

Hetsch stopped, wanting to go back to Finsterau. He'd get Afra to explain herself, he'd stay until she said yes, had to say yes. And if she didn't, then she wouldn't know what had hit her. A man like him wasn't going to turn up

again. What did she want, anyway? She should be glad
he was courting her. He'd soon show her that he couldn't
be treated like that. Not him! Yes, that was exactly what
he'd do.

Afra

The broken pieces of the vase are lying in the bedroom all over the place, including under the bed. Afra bends down and sweeps them up with the little brush. In her thoughts she is still with the child in the kitchen; she is afraid that in spite of her prohibition he might get up and run over to the stove. She keeps one ear open for any sound.

Where can her father be? It's late, he ought to be home any time now. She hears footsteps in the corridor, a little rustling, and then the kitchen door is opened. Afra is sure she recognizes her father's footsteps. She is relieved; that means that Albert isn't alone in the kitchen, her father will keep an eye on him.

Suddenly she hears the child crying. She leaves everything where it is and runs into the kitchen as fast as she can go. Hand still on the door handle, the door half open, she sees the little boy crouching on the floor beside the bench in the corner. Snot and tears are running down his face.

'What's the matter, Albert? Have you hurt yourself?'

Afra hurries towards him, bends down to comfort the crying child. Out of the corner of her eye she sees the person who is in the room with them. It is not her father. She turns her head to one side, sees the other travelling journeyman standing with his back to the dresser, the young fellow who reminded her of Albert's father yesterday. Afra doesn't understand what is going on, she thought she had recognized the sound of her father's footsteps, and then she sees the open doors and drawers. She straightens her back, stands up, takes a step towards the young man.

'What are you looking for there? Go away, go on, get out of here!'

He doesn't seem like someone caught out in a guilty act; he is calm, he even grins at her.

'What do you think I'm looking for? Money, something to eat, and whatever else I can find.'

'There's nothing to be found here. We don't have anything.'

Afra plucks up all her courage and goes on walking slowly towards him.

He moves a little way aside, and for a moment Afra thinks he is making room for her. Only then does she see the knife. He is holding it in the hand that had been hidden behind his back.

'If I were you I'd sit down on the bench here in this kitchen and keep quiet. Then nothing will happen to you or the child either.'

He says it with a smile, but his eyes and his voice are cold.

Afra hesitates, but then she goes on walking slowly his way.

'Put that knife away. You don't frighten me, I've dealt with worse than you before.'

She quickly darts at the young man, trying to seize his arm. He turns away, pushing her back with his shoulder. Afra tackles him. He takes her hair in his free hand. She tries to scratch him, bite him. He moves to fling her off. She clutches him, kicking out and trying to hit his shin. Finally she gets a grip on his arm.

For a moment they are both holding the knife in their hands; the young fellow won't let go and is trying to wrestle Afra to the floor. They collide with the kitchen dresser. The china in the cupboard clinks, the dresser doors slam back against its frame. Albert is screaming and crying. He scrambles up and runs to his mother. She finally succeeds in getting the knife away from the young man, cutting his hand as she does so.

'You just get out of here!'

Afra clutches the knife in both hands. She stands with her back to the kitchen door, never taking her eyes off the young man, holding him in check. Meanwhile, Albert is clinging to her skirt, a heavy weight.

'The bitch stabbed me! Look, I'm bleeding! You just wait, I'll show you!'

The journeyman is hardly more than an arm's length away from her. All she hears is Albert crying, she doesn't notice the second man until he swings back his arm and hits her over the head with a bottle. The knife falls to the floor. Afra staggers, is just in time to catch hold of the table. She tries to get back on her feet, struggles up, but then a second blow strikes her. The child's voice is breaking desperately as he tries to get closer to his mother. One of the two men grabs Albert, pulls him away, flings him carelessly into a corner like a rag doll, and he lies there whimpering. Afra clutches her attacker's legs. He kicks out at her, pushing her away. Strikes her again. With the last of her strength, Afra drags herself over to the sofa, clings to it with both hands and tries to pull herself up. Blood is running down her face.

She sees it only dimly when one of the two attackers pushes her down on the sofa and hits her yet again. Then everything goes black in front of her eyes.

**From the statement of
Matthias Karrer, pedlar and knife-grinder,
eighteen years after the events concerned**

When I realized that Wackes had escaped the
police, and there was only Otto and me left
to take the rap, the whole thing rankled.
I resented that Frenchman. First he talks
big, then he dumps us in the shit. Makes off
because he knows what's what — the hell he
does! And a man like that talks about the
Legion day and night, and how we need guts!
I told Otto what I thought of his friend,
I thought he was a bad lot, a windbag, not
an ounce of honesty in his body.

'He let us down when we needed him, that's
not right! That's a rotten thing to do.'

That's what I told Otto.

At first Otto wouldn't listen, told me to keep my mouth shut, but after a while he let out his own resentment of Wackes. He started telling me other things he'd done along with the Frenchman, how it wasn't the first time they'd climbed in somewhere, and how glad he really is to be rid of him.

'Wackes is a bastard. Tell you what, though, it has its good side that they caught me now, or I could have ended badly. So he's gone off, but you have to watch every word with him, every damn thing he says. He's fine one minute, the next he has a knife in his hand. You weren't the first to find that out.'

That's what he said to me.

And then, bit by bit, he told me about everything, all the time he was going around with Wackes. At first I didn't quite believe him, because when you're in the clink you hear all kinds of stories, and most of them aren't true.

We were in the same cell, see, and in the night, when Otto couldn't sleep, he kept on talking, telling his stories, specially the one that wouldn't let him rest, and that's how I found out all about it.

'Before we met you we came to that house, and that's where it happened. Over in the neighbourhood of Finsterau. At first it was like what we'd always done. I went into the house and asked if we could wash at the well out in the yard, and whether we could have a bite to eat. Of course I really went in to see what was to be had there. I'd be lying if I didn't say as much. So I went in on a pretext, to see who was in the house. But there was only the young woman and the child, I told Wackes, and then he went in after me. He still thought a woman like that is easy to intimidate, and if they had anything he'd get hold of it. Only he had to work fast in case anyone came along.'

Otto himself, he'd been supposed to wait outside the house by the well and keep watch in case anyone came. He didn't go in until he heard the noise they made scuffling.

'The child was yelling as if he was on the spit, and the woman stood there with the knife in her hand. Wackes had shouted that she'd cut his hand. So I didn't hesitate, I got hold of an empty bottle and I hit her with it. What else could I do? She dropped the knife and she just managed to catch hold of the table. Then Wackes took two or three steps towards her and pushed the knife away. But she kept going, she staggered up again, and then it all went very fast and Wackes hit her again. First with the bottle — he'd snatched it out of my hand — and then with a little hoe. How he came by that hoe so fast I can't say. I just stood there, I didn't move. Until Wackes yelled at me to get out and keep watch. Because if someone else comes along now, he says, we'd be for it. I went out into the yard and packed up our things. A couple more minutes and the Frenchman was out of there again, and we were off.'

Later, he said the Frenchman told him he'd fucked the woman again. And he hit the child with the hoe.

'On account of he wouldn't stop whining and whimpering.'

But Otto didn't want to hear that.

It wasn't worth it either, all they brought away was a dried sausage, a few marks and a pocket watch. He'd found the money and the watch in the bedroom after he hit her.

I couldn't forget that story. I wanted to know whether there was any truth in it, and if so what, or was it just all rubbish? And I wanted them to go looking for that bastard Wackes. That's why I told one of the warders about it. But he didn't believe me, he thought I just wanted to make trouble for someone else the way folk do, thinking I'd look better myself and have better cards to play when the bakery case came to court. And Otto, what a coward, of course next minute he said he knew nothing about it. He wouldn't even have owned up to knowing his own mother if they'd asked him. If he'd told all he knew he'd certainly have been for it.

When I got out of prison I hadn't thought of it again for years. How was I to know whether the story was true, or whether Otto had just made it up? I only found out later it was true, and only by chance on the road because I was in the Finsterau area. A customer told me about it, and it was from him I got the old press cutting.

And when I wanted to report it again nobody would believe me. They all said the 'real' murderer had been condemned to prison. Wackes was in the Legion, I suppose, and Otto, he never could cope with anything. Later he got stabbed in a tavern brawl. At least, that's what I heard.

But I never could forget the story of the young woman and her child.

Wackes

When Winfried Niedermayer drove the bus into the works yard at 4.30 after his last round, it had been a working day like any other. He'd come on duty in the morning, had a bite of lunch in the bus, took a little rest afterwards. Nothing else had happened that day.

He parked the bus according to the rules, took his jacket that was hanging behind the driver's seat, and picked up his bag. Looked around once more to make sure it was all in order, then he got out, locked the vehicle, and was going over to the office as usual to hand in the key and cross himself off the list.

The men were coming towards him just as he was going over the yard to the office. They had seen him even as he was driving the bus into the works, but he hadn't taken any notice of them. Now they asked what his name was, and whether he had been a journeyman roaming the country-side around Finsterau in the summer of 1947. Then he knew that they had come to take him away. All he said was that he'd been expecting them for a long time.

They arrested him. He took it all calmly and didn't defend himself.

When they asked him, later, 'Why the little boy as well?' he replied, 'When the cat dies you kill her litter too.'